Last Poems by A. E. Housman

Last Poems by A. E. Housman

by A. E. Housman

Copyright © 6/8/2015
Jefferson Publication

ISBN-13: 978-1514282694

Printed in the United States of America

All rights reserved. No part of this book may be reprinted or reproduced or utilized in any form or by any electronic, mechanical, or other means, now known or hereafter invented, including photocopying and recording, or in any form of storage or retrieval system, without prior permission in writing from the publisher.'

Contents

I. THE WEST 4
II. 5
III. 6
IV. ILLIC JACET 6
V. GRENADIER 7
VI. LANCER 8
VII. 8
VIII. 9
IX. 10
X. 11
XI. 11
XII. 11
XIII. THE DESERTER 12
XIV. THE CULPRIT 13
XV. EIGHT O'CLOCK 14
XVI. SPRING MORNING 14
XVII. ASTRONOMY 15
XVIII. 16
XIX. 17
XX. 17
XXI. 18
XXII. 18
XXIII. 19
XXIV. EPITHALAMIUM 19
XXV. THE ORACLES 20
XXVI. 21
XXVII. 21
XXVIII. 21
XXIX. 22
XXX. SINNER'S RUE 23
XXXI. HELL'S GATE 23
XXXII. 26
XXXIII. 26

XXXIV.	27
XXXV.	28
XXXVI. REVOLUTION	28
XXXVII. EPITAPH ON AN ARMY OF MERCENARIES	29
XXXVIII.	29
XXXIX.	30
XL.	31
XLI. FANCY'S KNELL	32

I. THE WEST

Beyond the moor and the mountain crest
—Comrade, look not on the west—
The sun is down and drinks away
From air and land the lees of day.

The long cloud and the single pine
Sentinel the ending line,
And out beyond it, clear and wan,
Reach the gulfs of evening on.

The son of woman turns his brow
West from forty countries now,
And, as the edge of heaven he eyes,
Thinks eternal thoughts, and sighs.

Oh wide's the world, to rest or roam,
With change abroad and cheer at home,
Fights and furloughs, talk and tale,
Company and beef and ale.

But if I front the evening sky
Silent on the west look I,
And my comrade, stride for stride,
Paces silent at my side,

Comrade, look not on the west:
'Twill have the heart out of your breast;
'Twill take your thoughts and sink them far,
Leagues beyond the sunset bar.

Oh lad, I fear that yon's the sea
Where they fished for you and me,

And there, from whence we both were ta'en,
You and I shall drown again.

Send not on your soul before
To dive from that beguiling shore,
And let not yet the swimmer leave
His clothes upon the sands of eve.

Too fast to yonder strand forlorn
We journey, to the sunken bourn,
To flush the fading tinges eyed
By other lads at eventide.

Wide is the world, to rest or roam,
And early 'tis for turning home:
Plant your heel on earth and stand,
And let's forget our native land.

When you and I are split on air
Long we shall be strangers there;
Friends of flesh and bone are best;
Comrade, look not on the west.

II.

As I gird on for fighting
   My sword upon my thigh,
I think on old ill fortunes
   Of better men than I.

Think I, the round world over,
   What golden lads are low
With hurts not mine to mourn for
   And shames I shall not know.

What evil luck soever
   For me remains in store,
'Tis sure much finer fellows
   Have fared much worse before.

So here are things to think on

That ought to make me brave,
As I strap on for fighting
  My sword that will not save.

III.

Her strong enchantments failing,
  Her towers of fear in wreck,
Her limbecks dried of poisons
  And the knife at her neck,

The Queen of air and darkness
  Begins to shrill and cry,
'O young man, O my slayer,
  To-morrow you shall die.'

O Queen of air and darkness,
  I think 'tis truth you say,
And I shall die to-morrow;
  But you will die to-day.

IV. ILLIC JACET

Oh hard is the bed they have made him,
  And common the blanket and cheap;
But there he will lie as they laid him:
  Where else could you trust him to sleep?

To sleep when the bugle is crying
  And cravens have heard and are brave,
When mothers and sweethearts are sighing
  And lads are in love with the grave.

Oh dark is the chamber and lonely,
  And lights and companions depart;
But lief will he lose them and only

Behold the desire of his heart.

And low is the roof, but it covers
    A sleeper content to repose;
And far from his friends and his lovers
    He lies with the sweetheart he chose.

V. GRENADIER

The Queen she sent to look for me,
    The sergeant he did say,
'Young man, a soldier will you be
    For thirteen pence a day?'

For thirteen pence a day did I
    Take off the things I wore,
And I have marched to where I lie,
    And I shall march no more.

My mouth is dry, my shirt is wet,
    My blood runs all away,
So now I shall not die in debt
    For thirteen pence a day.

To-morrow after new young men
    The sergeant he must see,
For things will all be over then
    Between the Queen and me.

And I shall have to bate my price,
    For in the grave, they say,
Is neither knowledge nor device
    Nor thirteen pence a day.

VI. LANCER

I 'listed at home for a lancer,
   Oh who would not sleep with the brave?
I 'listed at home for a lancer
   To ride on a horse to my grave.

And over the seas we were bidden
   A country to take and to keep;
And far with the brave I have ridden,
   And now with the brave I shall sleep.

For round me the men will be lying
   That learned me the way to behave.
And showed me my business of dying:
   Oh who would not sleep with the brave?

They ask and there is not an answer;
Says I, I will 'list for a lancer,
   Oh who would not sleep with the brave?

And I with the brave shall be sleeping
   At ease on my mattress of loam,
When back from their taking and keeping
   The squadron is riding home.

The wind with the plumes will be playing,
   The girls will stand watching them wave,
And eyeing my comrades and saying
   Oh who would not sleep with the brave?

They ask and there is not an answer;
Says you, I will 'list for a lancer,
   Oh who would not sleep with the brave?

VII.

In valleys green and still
   Where lovers wander maying
They hear from over hill

A music playing.

Behind the drum and fife,
   Past hawthornwood and hollow,
Through earth and out of life
   The soldiers follow.

The soldier's is the trade:
   In any wind or weather
He steals the heart of maid
   And man together.

The lover and his lass
   Beneath the hawthorn lying
Have heard the soldiers pass,
   And both are sighing.

And down the distance they
   With dying note and swelling
Walk the resounding way
   To the still dwelling.

VIII.

Soldier from the wars returning,
   Spoiler of the taken town,
Here is ease that asks not earning;
   Turn you in and sit you down.

Peace is come and wars are over,
   Welcome you and welcome all,
While the charger crops the clover
   And his bridle hangs in stall.

Now no more of winters biting,
   Filth in trench from fall to spring,
Summers full of sweat and fighting
   For the Kesar or the King.

Rest you, charger, rust you, bridle;
   Kings and kesars, keep your pay;

Soldier, sit you down and idle
  At the inn of night for aye.

IX.

The chestnut casts his flambeaux, and the flowers
  Stream from the hawthorn on the wind away,
The doors clap to, the pane is blind with showers.
  Pass me the can, lad; there's an end of May.

There's one spoilt spring to scant our mortal lot,
  One season ruined of our little store.
May will be fine next year as like as not:
  Oh ay, but then we shall be twenty-four.

We for a certainty are not the first
  Have sat in taverns while the tempest hurled
Their hopeful plans to emptiness, and cursed
  Whatever brute and blackguard made the world.

It is in truth iniquity on high
  To cheat our sentenced souls of aught they crave,
And mar the merriment as you and I
  Fare on our long fool's-errand to the grave.

Iniquity it is; but pass the can.
  My lad, no pair of kings our mothers bore;
Our only portion is the estate of man:
  We want the moon, but we shall get no more.

If here to-day the cloud of thunder lours
  To-morrow it will hie on far behests;
The flesh will grieve on other bones than ours
  Soon, and the soul will mourn in other breasts.

The troubles of our proud and angry dust
  Are from eternity, and shall not fail.
Bear them we can, and if we can we must.
  Shoulder the sky, my lad, and drink your ale.

X.

Could man be drunk for ever
   With liquor, love, or fights,
Lief should I rouse at morning
   And lief lie down of nights.

But men at whiles are sober
   And think by fits and starts,
And if they think, they fasten
   Their hands upon their hearts.

XI.

Yonder see the morning blink:
   The sun is up, and up must I,
To wash and dress and eat and drink
And look at things and talk and think
   And work, and God knows why.

Oh often have I washed and dressed
   And what's to show for all my pain?
Let me lie abed and rest:
Ten thousand times I've done my best
   And all's to do again.

XII.

   The laws of God, the laws of man,
He may keep that will and can;

Now I: let God and man decree
Laws for themselves and not for me;
And if my ways are not as theirs
Let them mind their own affairs.
Their deeds I judge and much condemn,
Yet when did I make laws for them?
Please yourselves, say I, and they
Need only look the other way.
But no, they will not; they must still
Wrest their neighbour to their will,
And make me dance as they desire
With jail and gallows and hell-fire.
And how am I to face the odds
Of man's bedevilment and God's?
I, a stranger and afraid
In a world I never made.
They will be master, right or wrong;
Though both are foolish, both are strong,
And since, my soul, we cannot fly
To Saturn or Mercury,
Keep we must, if keep we can,
These foreign laws of God and man.

XIII. THE DESERTER

"What sound awakened me, I wonder,
   For now 'tis dumb."
"Wheels on the road most like, or thunder:
   Lie down; 'twas not the drum.:

"Toil at sea and two in haven
   And trouble far:
Fly, crow, away, and follow, raven,
   And all that croaks for war."

"Hark, I heard the bugle crying,
   And where am I?
My friends are up and dressed and dying,
   And I will dress and die."

"Oh love is rare and trouble plenty

And carrion cheap,
And daylight dear at four-and-twenty:
   Lie down again and sleep."

"Reach me my belt and leave your prattle:
   Your hour is gone;
But my day is the day of battle,
   And that comes dawning on.

"They mow the field of man in season:
   Farewell, my fair,
And, call it truth or call it treason,
   Farewell the vows that were."

"Ay, false heart, forsake me lightly:
   'Tis like the brave.
They find no bed to joy in rightly
   Before they find the grave.

"Their love is for their own undoing.
   And east and west
They scour about the world a-wooing
   The bullet in their breast.

"Sail away the ocean over,
   Oh sail away,
And lie there with your leaden lover
   For ever and a day."

XIV. THE CULPRIT

The night my father got me
   His mind was not on me;
He did not plague his fancy
   To muse if I should be
   The son you see.

The day my mother bore me
   She was a fool and glad,
For all the pain I cost her,
   That she had borne the lad

That borne she had.

My mother and my father
   Out of the light they lie;
The warrant would not find them,
   And here 'tis only I
   Shall hang so high.

Oh let not man remember
   The soul that God forgot,
But fetch the county kerchief
   And noose me in the knot,
   And I will rot.

For so the game is ended
   That should not have begun.
My father and my mother
   They had a likely son,
   And I have none.

XV. EIGHT O'CLOCK

He stood, and heard the steeple
   Sprinkle the quarters on the morning town.
One, two, three, four, to market-place and people
   It tossed them down.

Strapped, noosed, nighing his hour,
   He stood and counted them and cursed his luck;
And then the clock collected in the tower
   Its strength, and struck.

XVI. SPRING MORNING

Star and coronal and bell
   April underfoot renews,

And the hope of man as well
  Flowers among the morning dews.

Now the old come out to look,
  Winter past and winter's pains.
How the sky in pool and brook
  Glitters on the grassy plains.

Easily the gentle air
  Wafts the turning season on;
Things to comfort them are there,
  Though 'tis true the best are gone.

Now the scorned unlucky lad
  Rousing from his pillow gnawn
Mans his heart and deep and glad
  Drinks the valiant air of dawn.

Half the night he longed to die,
  Now are sown on hill and plain
Pleasures worth his while to try
  Ere he longs to die again.

Blue the sky from east to west
  Arches, and the world is wide,
Though the girl he loves the best
  Rouses from another's side.

XVII. ASTRONOMY

The Wain upon the northern steep
  Descends and lifts away.
Oh I will sit me down and weep
  For bones in Africa.

For pay and medals, name and rank,
  Things that he has not found,
He hove the Cross to heaven and sank
  The pole-star underground.

And now he does not even see

Signs of the nadir roll
At night over the ground where he
  Is buried with the pole.

XVIII.

The rain, it streams on stone and hillock,
  The boot clings to the clay.
Since all is done that's due and right
Let's home; and now, my lad, good-night,
  For I must turn away.

Good-night, my lad, for nought's eternal;
  No league of ours, for sure.
Tomorrow I shall miss you less,
And ache of heart and heaviness
  Are things that time should cure.

Over the hill the highway marches
  And what's beyond is wide:
Oh soon enough will pine to nought
Remembrance and the faithful thought
  That sits the grave beside.

The skies, they are not always raining
  Nor grey the twelvemonth through;
And I shall meet good days and mirth,
And range the lovely lands of earth
  With friends no worse than you.

But oh, my man, the house is fallen
  That none can build again;
My man, how full of joy and woe
Your mother bore you years ago
  To-night to lie in the rain.

XIX.

In midnights of November,
 When Dead Man's Fair is nigh,
And danger in the valley,
 And anger in the sky,

Around the huddling homesteads
 The leafless timber roars,
And the dead call the dying
 And finger at the doors.

Oh, yonder faltering fingers
 Are hands I used to hold;
Their false companion drowses
 And leaves them in the cold.

Oh, to the bed of ocean,
 To Africk and to Ind,
I will arise and follow
 Along the rainy wind.

The night goes out and under
 With all its train forlorn;
Hues in the east assemble
 And cocks crow up the morn.

The living are the living
 And dead the dead will stay,
And I will sort with comrades
 That face the beam of day.

XX.

The night is freezing fast,
 To-morrow comes December;
  And winterfalls of old
Are with me from the past;
 And chiefly I remember
  How Dick would hate the cold.

Fall, winter, fall; for he,
   Prompt hand and headpiece clever,
      Has woven a winter robe,
And made of earth and sea
   His overcoat for ever,
      And wears the turning globe.

XXI.

The fairies break their dances
   And leave the printed lawn,
And up from India glances
   The silver sail of dawn.

The candles burn their sockets,
   The blinds let through the day,
The young man feels his pockets
   And wonders what's to pay.

XXII.

The sloe was lost in flower,
   The April elm was dim;
That was the lover's hour,
   The hour for lies and him.

If thorns are all the bower,
   If north winds freeze the fir,
Why, 'tis another's hour,
   The hour for truth and her.

XXIII.

In the morning, in the morning,
   In the happy field of hay,
Oh they looked at one another
   By the light of day.

In the blue and silver morning
   On the haycock as they lay,
Oh they looked at one another
   And they looked away.

XXIV. EPITHALAMIUM

   He is here, Urania's son,
Hymen come from Helicon;
God that glads the lover's heart,
He is here to join and part.
So the groomsman quits your side
And the bridegroom seeks the bride:
Friend and comrade yield you o'er
To her that hardly loves you more.

   Now the sun his skyward beam
Has tilted from the Ocean stream.
Light the Indies, laggard sun:
Happy bridegroom, day is done,
And the star from OEta's steep
Calls to bed but not to sleep.

   Happy bridegroom, Hesper brings
All desired and timely things.
All whom morning sends to roam,
Hesper loves to lead them home.
Home return who him behold,
Child to mother, sheep to fold,
Bird to nest from wandering wide:
Happy bridegroom, seek your bride.

   Pour it out, the golden cup

Given and guarded, brimming up,
Safe through jostling markets borne
And the thicket of the thorn;
Folly spurned and danger past,
Pour it to the god at last.

   Now, to smother noise and light,
Is stolen abroad the wildering night,
And the blotting shades confuse
Path and meadow full of dews;
And the high heavens, that all control,
Turn in silence round the pole.
Catch the starry beams they shed
Prospering the marriage bed,
And breed the land that reared your prime
Sons to stay the rot of time.
All is quiet, no alarms;
Nothing fear of nightly harms.
Safe you sleep on guarded ground,
And in silent circle round
The thoughts of friends keep watch and ward,
Harnessed angels, hand on sword.

XXV. THE ORACLES

'Tis mute, the word they went to hear on high Dodona mountain
   When winds were in the oakenshaws and all the cauldrons tolled,
And mute's the midland navel-stone beside the singing fountain,
   And echoes list to silence now where gods told lies of old.

I took my question to the shrine that has not ceased from speaking,
   The heart within, that tells the truth and tells it twice as plain;
And from the cave of oracles I heard the priestess shrieking
   That she and I should surely die and never live again.

Oh priestess, what you cry is clear, and sound good sense I think it;
   But let the screaming echoes rest, and froth your mouth no more.
'Tis true there's better boose than brine, but he that drowns must drink it;
   And oh, my lass, the news is news that men have heard before.

The King with half the East at heel is marched from lands of morning;

Their fighters drink the rivers up, their shafts benight the air.
And he that stands will die for nought, and home there's no returning.
The Spartans on the sea-wet rock sat down and combed their hair.

XXVI.

The half-moon westers low, my love,
    And the wind brings up the rain;
And wide apart lie we, my love,
    And seas between the twain.

I know not if it rains, my love,
    In the land where you do lie;
And oh, so sound you sleep, my love,
    You know no more than I.

XXVII.

The sigh that heaves the grasses
    Whence thou wilt never rise
Is of the air that passes
    And knows not if it sighs.

The diamond tears adorning
    Thy low mound on the lea,
Those are the tears of morning,
    That weeps, but not for thee.

XXVIII.

Now dreary dawns the eastern light,

And fall of eve is drear,
And cold the poor man lies at night,
   And so goes out the year.

Little is the luck I've had,
   And oh, 'tis comfort small
To think that many another lad
   Has had no luck at all.

XXIX.

Wake not for the world-heard thunder
   Nor the chime that earthquakes toll.
Star may plot in heaven with planet,
Lightning rive the rock of granite,
Tempest tread the oakwood under:
   Fear not you for flesh nor soul.
Marching, fighting, victory past,
Stretch your limbs in peace at last.

Stir not for the soldiers drilling
   Nor the fever nothing cures:
Throb of drum and timbal's rattle
Call but man alive to battle,
And the fife with death-notes filling
   Screams for blood but not for yours.
Times enough you bled your best;
Sleep on now, and take your rest.

Sleep, my lad; the French are landed,
   London's burning, Windsor's down;
Clasp your cloak of earth about you,
We must man the ditch without you,
March unled and fight short-handed,
   Charge to fall and swim to drown.
Duty, friendship, bravery o'er,
Sleep away, lad; wake no more.

XXX. SINNER'S RUE

I walked alone and thinking,
   And faint the nightwind blew
And stirred on mounds at crossways
   The flower of sinner's rue.

Where the roads part they bury
   Him that his own hand slays,
And so the weed of sorrow
   Springs at the four cross ways.

By night I plucked it hueless,
   When morning broke 'twas blue:
Blue at my breast I fastened
   The flower of sinner's rue.

It seemed a herb of healing,
   A balsam and a sign,
Flower of a heart whose trouble
   Must have been worse than mine.

Dead clay that did me kindness,
   I can do none to you,
But only wear for breastknot
   The flower of sinner's rue.

XXXI. HELL'S GATE

   Onward led the road again
Through the sad uncoloured plain
Under twilight brooding dim,
And along the utmost rim
Wall and rampart risen to sight
Cast a shadow not of night,
And beyond them seemed to glow
Bonfires lighted long ago.
And my dark conductor broke
Silence at my side and spoke,
Saying, "You conjecture well:

Yonder is the gate of hell."

   Ill as yet the eye could see
The eternal masonry,
But beneath it on the dark
To and fro there stirred a spark.
And again the sombre guide
Knew my question, and replied:
"At hell gate the damned in turn
Pace for sentinel and burn."

   Dully at the leaden sky
Staring, and with idle eye
Measuring the listless plain,
I began to think again.
Many things I thought of then,
Battle, and the loves of men,
Cities entered, oceans crossed,
Knowledge gained and virtue lost,
Cureless folly done and said,
And the lovely way that led
To the slimepit and the mire
And the everlasting fire.
And against a smoulder dun
And a dawn without a sun
Did the nearing bastion loom,
And across the gate of gloom
Still one saw the sentry go,
Trim and burning, to and fro,
One for women to admire
In his finery of fire.
Something, as I watched him pace,
Minded me of time and place,
Soldiers of another corps
And a sentry known before.

   Ever darker hell on high
Reared its strength upon the sky,
And our footfall on the track
Fetched the daunting echo back.
But the soldier pacing still
The insuperable sill,
Nursing his tormented pride,
Turned his head to neither side,
Sunk into himself apart
And the hell-fire of his heart.

But against our entering in
From the drawbridge Death and Sin
Rose to render key and sword
To their father and their lord.
And the portress foul to see
Lifted up her eyes on me
Smiling, and I made reply:
"Met again, my lass," said I.
Then the sentry turned his head,
Looked, and knew me, and was Ned.

   Once he looked, and halted straight,
Set his back against the gate,
Caught his musket to his chin,
While the hive of hell within
Sent abroad a seething hum
As of towns whose king is come
Leading conquest home from far
And the captives of his war,
And the car of triumph waits,
And they open wide the gates.
But across the entry barred
Straddled the revolted guard,
Weaponed and accoutred well
From the arsenals of hell;
And beside him, sick and white,
Sin to left and Death to right
Turned a countenance of fear
On the flaming mutineer.
Over us the darkness bowed,
And the anger in the cloud
Clenched the lightning for the stroke;
But the traitor musket spoke.

   And the hollowness of hell
Sounded as its master fell,
And the mourning echo rolled
Ruin through his kingdom old.
Tyranny and terror flown
Left a pair of friends alone,
And beneath the nether sky
All that stirred was he and I.

   Silent, nothing found to say,
We began the backward way;
And the ebbing luster died

From the soldier at my side,
As in all his spruce attire
Failed the everlasting fire.
Midmost of the homeward track
Once we listened and looked back;
But the city, dusk and mute,
Slept, and there was no pursuit.

XXXII.

When I would muse in boyhood
    The wild green woods among,
And nurse resolves and fancies
    Because the world was young,
It was not foes to conquer,
    Nor sweethearts to be kind,
But it was friends to die for
    That I would seek and find.

I sought them far and found them,
    The sure, the straight, the brave,
The hearts I lost my own to,
    The souls I could not save.
They braced their belts about them,
    They crossed in ships the sea,
They sought and found six feet of ground,
    And there they died for me.

XXXIII.

When the eye of day is shut,
    And the stars deny their beams,
And about the forest hut
    Blows the roaring wood of dreams,

From deep clay, from desert rock,

From the sunk sands of the main,
Come not at my door to knock,
   Hearts that loved me not again.

Sleep, be still, turn to your rest
   In the lands where you are laid;
In far lodgings east and west
   Lie down on the beds you made.

In gross marl, in blowing dust,
   In the drowned ooze of the sea,
Where you would not, lie you must,
   Lie you must, and not with me.

XXXIV.

THE FIRST OF MAY
The orchards half the way
   From home to Ludlow fair
Flowered on the first of May
   In Mays when I was there;
And seen from stile or turning
   The plume of smoke would show
Where fires were burning
   That went out long ago.

The plum broke forth in green,
   The pear stood high and snowed,
My friends and I between
   Would take the Ludlow road;
Dressed to the nines and drinking
   And light in heart and limb,
And each chap thinking
   The fair was held for him.

Between the trees in flower
   New friends at fairtime tread
The way where Ludlow tower
   Stands planted on the dead.
Our thoughts, a long while after,
   They think, our words they say;

Theirs now's the laughter,
    The fair, the first of May.

Ay, yonder lads are yet
    The fools that we were then;
For oh, the sons we get
    Are still the sons of men.
The sumless tale of sorrow
    Is all unrolled in vain:
May comes to-morrow
    And Ludlow fair again.

XXXV.

When first my way to fair I took
    Few pence in purse had I,
And long I used to stand and look
    At things I could not buy.

Now times are altered: if I care
    To buy a thing, I can;
The pence are here and here's the fair,
    But where's the lost young man?

—To think that two and two are four
    And neither five nor three
The heart of man has long been sore
    And long 'tis like to be.

XXXVI. REVOLUTION

West and away the wheels of darkness roll,
    Day's beamy banner up the east is borne,
Spectres and fears, the nightmare and her foal,
    Drown in the golden deluge of the morn.

But over sea and continent from sight
   Safe to the Indies has the earth conveyed
The vast and moon-eclipsing cone of night,
   Her towering foolscap of eternal shade.

See, in mid heaven the sun is mounted; hark,
   The belfries tingle to the noonday chime.
'Tis silent, and the subterranean dark
   Has crossed the nadir, and begins to climb.

XXXVII. EPITAPH ON AN ARMY OF MERCENARIES

These, in the day when heaven was falling,
   The hour when earth's foundations fled,
Followed their mercenary calling
   And took their wages and are dead.

Their shoulders held the sky suspended;
   They stood, and earth's foundations stay;
What God abandoned, these defended,
   And saved the sum of things for pay.

XXXVIII.

Oh stay at home, my lad, and plough
   The land and not the sea,
And leave the soldiers at their drill,
And all about the idle hill
   Shepherd your sheep with me.

Oh stay with company and mirth
   And daylight and the air;
Too full already is the grave
Of fellows that were good and brave
   And died because they were.

XXXIX.

When summer's end is nighing
   And skies at evening cloud,
I muse on change and fortune
   And all the feats I vowed
   When I was young and proud.

The weathercock at sunset
   Would lose the slanted ray,
And I would climb the beacon
   That looked to Wales away
   And saw the last of day.

From hill and cloud and heaven
   The hues of evening died;
Night welled through lane and hollow
   And hushed the countryside,
   But I had youth and pride.

And I with earth and nightfall
   In converse high would stand,
Late, till the west was ashen
   And darkness hard at hand,
   And the eye lost the land.

The year might age, and cloudy
   The lessening day might close,
But air of other summers
   Breathed from beyond the snows,
   And I had hope of those.

They came and were and are not
   And come no more anew;
And all the years and seasons
   That ever can ensue
   Must now be worse and few.

So here's an end of roaming
   On eves when autumn nighs:

The ear too fondly listens
   For summer's parting sighs,
   And then the heart replies.

XL.

Tell me not here, it needs not saying,
   What tune the enchantress plays
In aftermaths of soft September
   Or under blanching mays,
For she and I were long acquainted
   And I knew all her ways.

On russet floors, by waters idle,
   The pine lets fall its cone;
The cuckoo shouts all day at nothing
   In leafy dells alone;
And traveler's joy beguiles in autumn
   Hearts that have lost their own.

On acres of the seeded grasses
   The changing burnish heaves;
Or marshalled under moons of harvest
   Stand still all night the sheaves;
Or beeches strip in storms for winter
   And stain the wind with leaves.

Possess, as I possessed a season,
   The countries I resign,
Where over elmy plains the highway
   Would mount the hills and shine,
And full of shade the pillared forest
   Would murmur and be mine.

For nature, heartless, witless nature,
   Will neither care nor know
What stranger's feet may find the meadow
   And trespass there and go,
Nor ask amid the dews of morning
   If they are mine or no.

XLI. FANCY'S KNELL

When lads were home from labour
    At Abdon under Clee,
A man would call his neighbor
    And both would send for me.
And where the light in lances
    Across the mead was laid,
There to the dances
    I fetched my flute and played.

Ours were idle pleasures,
    Yet oh, content we were,
The young to wind the measures,
    The old to heed the air;
And I to lift with playing
    From tree and tower and steep
The light delaying,
    And flute the sun to sleep.

The youth toward his fancy
    Would turn his brow of tan,
And Tom would pair with Nancy
    And Dick step off with Fan;
The girl would lift her glances
    To his, and both be mute:
Well went the dances
    At evening to the flute.

Wenlock Edge was umbered,
    And bright was Abdon Burf,
And warm between them slumbered
    The smooth green miles of turf;
Until from grass and clover
    The upshot beam would fade,
And England over
    Advanced the lofty shade.

The lofty shade advances,
    I fetch my flute and play:

Come, lads, and learn the dances
   And praise the tune to-day.
To-morrow, more's the pity,
   Away we both must hie,
To air the ditty,
   And to earth I.

Made in the USA
Las Vegas, NV
11 October 2025